C000156452

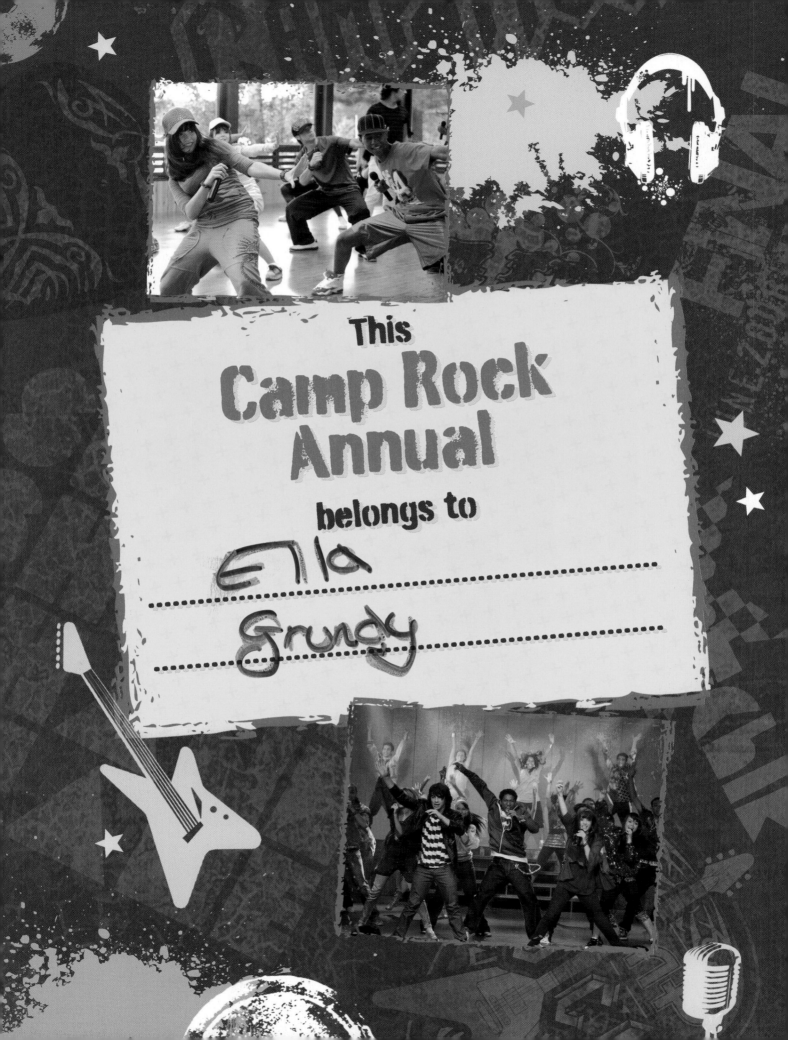

This
Camp Rock Annual
belongs to

Ella

Grundy

CAMP ROCK

ANNUAL 2010

Contents

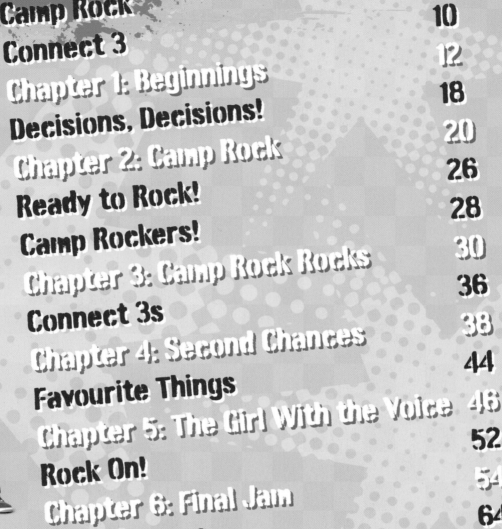
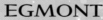

Camp Rock	8
Connect 3	10
Chapter 1: Beginnings	12
Decisions, Decisions!	18
Chapter 2: Camp Rock	20
Ready to Rock!	26
Camp Rockers!	28
Chapter 3: Camp Rock Rocks	30
Connect 3s	36
Chapter 4: Second Chances	38
Favourite Things	44
Chapter 5: The Girl With the Voice	46
Rock On!	52
Chapter 6: Final Jam	54
Get Creative!	64
Camp Rock Questions	66
A Message For You	68

EGMONT

We bring stories to life

First published in Great Britain in 2009 by Egmont UK Limited
239 Kensington High Street, London W8 6SA
Created for Egmont by Ruby Shoes Limited
Written by Brenda Apsley. Designed by Jeannette O'Toole.

Based on "Camp Rock" written by Karin Gist & Regina Hicks and
Julie Brown & Paul Brown © 2009 Disney Enterprises, Inc. All rights reserved.

ISBN 978 1 4052 4652 1
1 3 5 7 9 10 8 6 4 2
Printed in Italy

All rights reserved. No part of this publication may be reproduced, stored in a retrieval system, or transmitted, in any form or by any means, electronic, mechanical, photocopying, recording or otherwise, without the prior permission of the publisher and copyright owner.

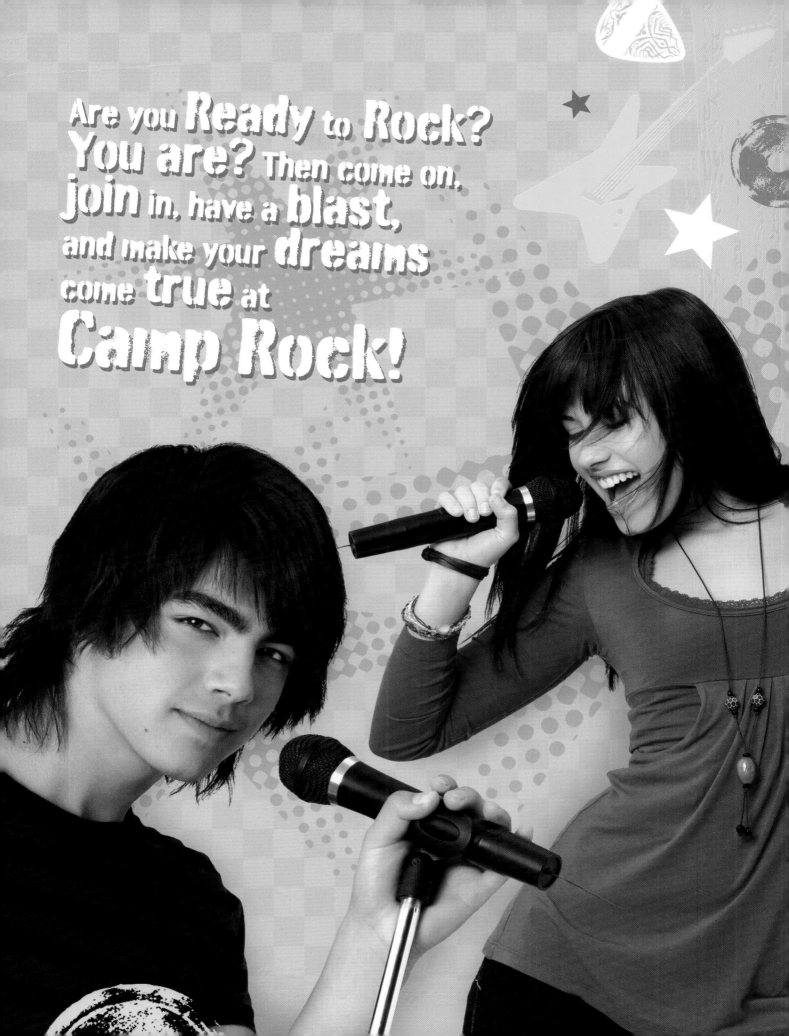

CAMP ROCK

... is where kids go to meet friends, make music – and hope their **dreams come true!**

Caitlyn

her passion
music producing and arranging
she loves
playing the keyboards
her fave music style
produced tunes

Tess

her passion
singing, dancing and performing
she loves
herself!
her fave music style
her own!

Mitchie

her passion
songwriting
she loves
meeting new people and having fun
her fave music style
she's open to everything

8

Barron

his passion
perfecting reggaeton rhymes
he loves
hanging with friends, especially Sander
his fave music style
reggaeton

Sander

his passion
performing and making people laugh
he loves
music, and hanging out with Barron
his fave music style
reggaeton

Peggy

her passion
Camp Rock
she loves
singing and dancing
her fave music style
anything she can sing and dance along to

Ella

her passion
singing and dancing
she loves
hanging out with Tess and Peggy
her fave music style
anything by Tess

CONNECT 3

Camp Rock is the summer music camp where, for some of the campers, dreams really do come true! It happened for Connect 3, and it can happen for you!

Let's meet Connect 3!

Shane - vocals

Shane, Nate and Jason had always made music together, but it all really started happening for them at Camp Rock.

Nate - guitar

Camp Rock got the boys noticed, and now they have a recording contract and hit records.

Jason - guitar

Jason, Shane and Nate used to come to Camp Rock every summer. It's where they found their sound.

CHAPTER 1
Beginnings

It was a big day for singer-songwriter Mitchie Torres. It was her last day at school before the summer break, and she was hoping to hear whether or not she'd be going to Camp Rock.

"Mitchie! Up! Last day of school!"

When Mitchie's mom, Connie, gave her a wake-up call, Mitchie's hand came out from under the duvet. She slid a CD into the player by her bedside, pressed play, then leapt out of bed.

The CD was labelled:

Mitchie's Tunes

and the words and music of her first song

Who Will I Be?

filled the room.

Mitchie sang along, then she smiled as she took out a notebook with

Mitchie's Songs

written on the cover, and scribbled down some new lyrics.

It was time to get ready for school, and Mitchie faced the big decision she had to take every morning ...

what to wear?

sunglasses?

bright red?

moody blue?

sunshine yellow?

no sunglasses?

beads?

bangles?

bracelets?

mini dress
and belt?

cap?

no cap?

high
heels?

boots?

flats?

Finally, she threw on a blue top, braided bangles and skinny jeans.

Mitchie picked up her guitar, strummed a few chords, then headed down for breakfast.

The top story on TV news programme *Hot Tunes* was about **Connect 3** singer, **Shane Gray**, who had walked off the set of the band's new video just because someone brought him the wrong kind of coffee.

"Word is that the other members of the band are fed up with Shane," said the reporter. "This stunt has cost the record label thousands of dollars, and it may cost the band their record deal. The message is clear: Shane Gray needs to clean up his act, and to give him time to do that, the mega, sell-out Connect 3 summer tour has been cancelled ..."

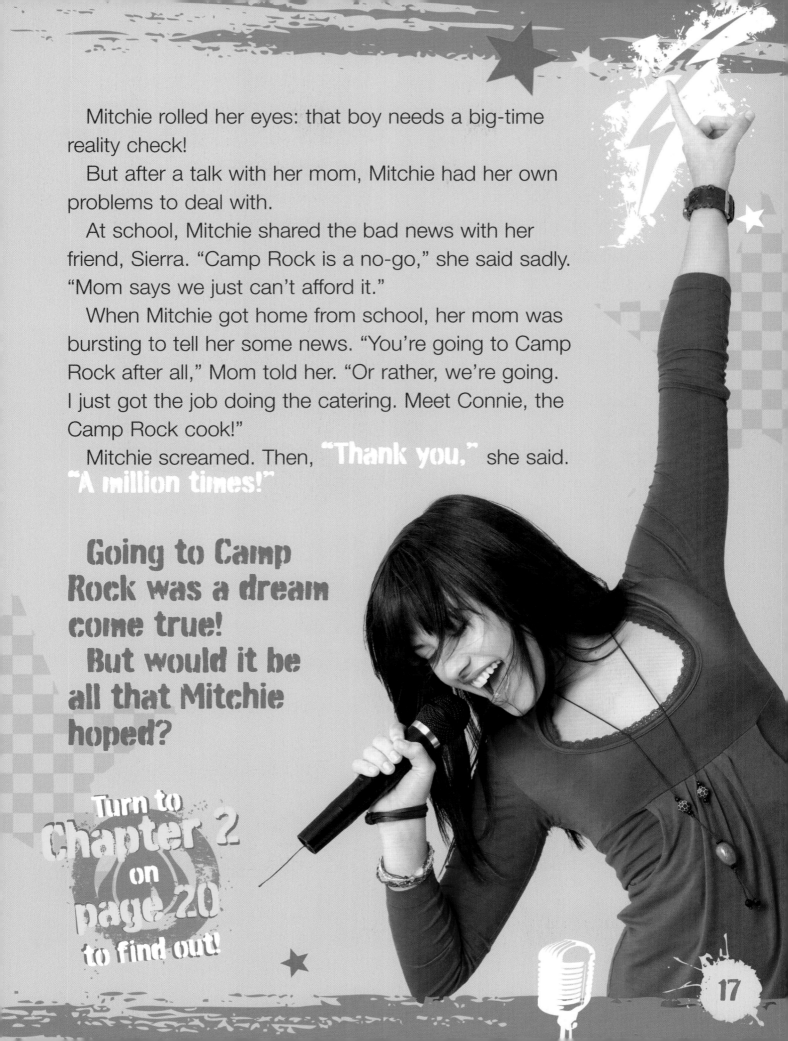

Mitchie rolled her eyes: that boy needs a big-time reality check!

But after a talk with her mom, Mitchie had her own problems to deal with.

At school, Mitchie shared the bad news with her friend, Sierra. "Camp Rock is a no-go," she said sadly. "Mom says we just can't afford it."

When Mitchie got home from school, her mom was bursting to tell her some news. "You're going to Camp Rock after all," Mom told her. "Or rather, we're going. I just got the job doing the catering. Meet Connie, the Camp Rock cook!"

Mitchie screamed. Then, **"Thank you,"** she said. **"A million times!"**

Going to Camp Rock was a dream come true!
But would it be all that Mitchie hoped?

Turn to **Chapter 2** on **page 20** to find out!

Decisions, Decisions!

It's Mitchie's big decision every morning – what's a girl going to wear? Rate Mitchie's choices by colouring in a number of stars for each one. Give the look you like best 5 stars, and award fewer stars for the others.

Can you design a great new look for Mitchie?
Draw and colour in your own 5-star outfit!
Why not try a mix of plain colours and patterns,
like these?

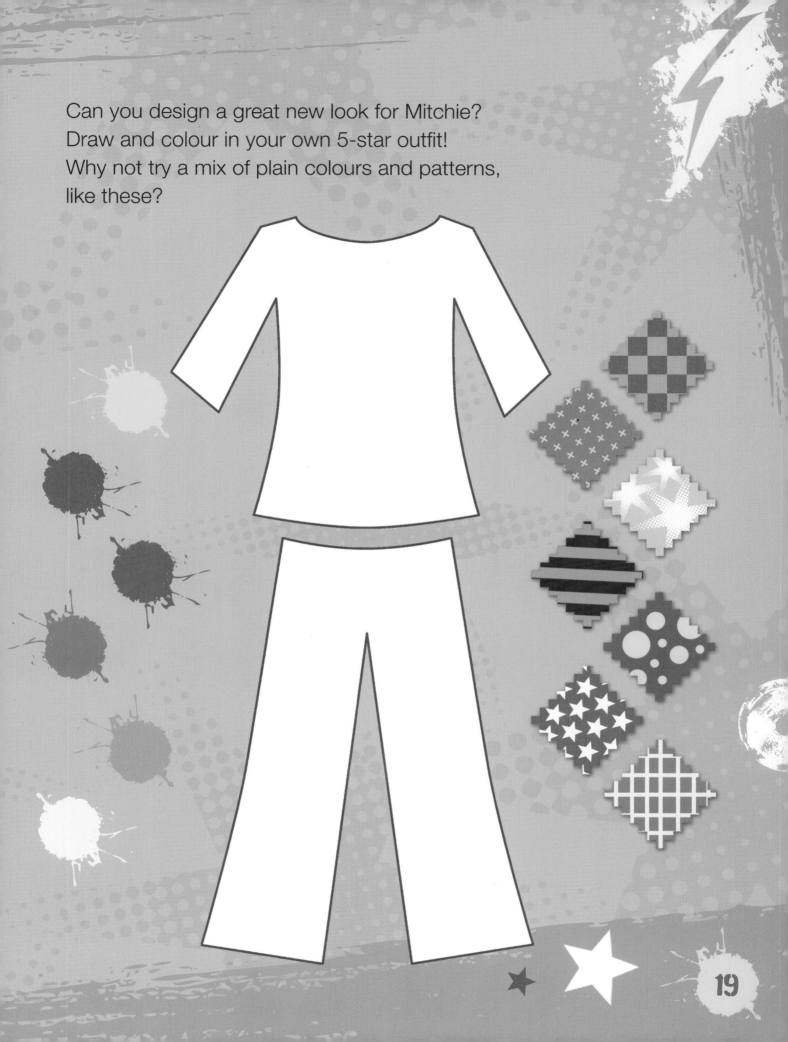

CHAPTER 2
Camp Rock

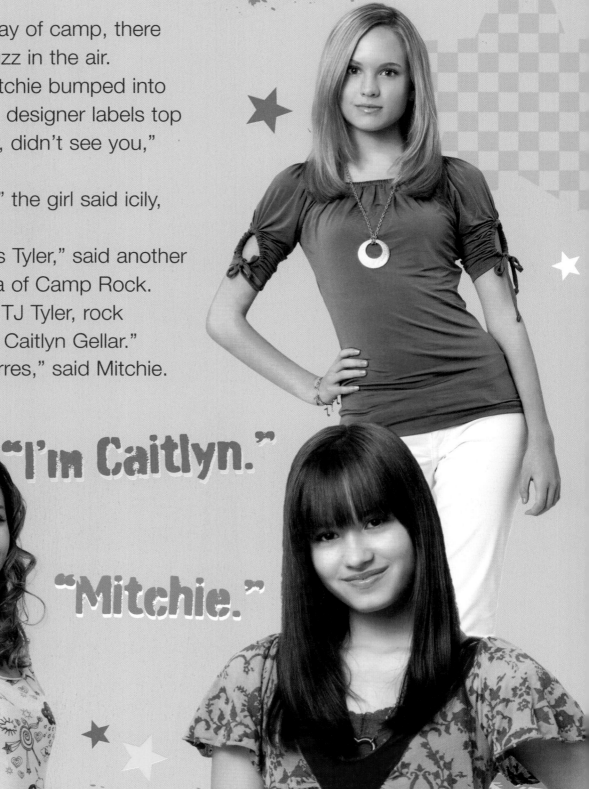

On the first day of camp, there was a real buzz in the air.

Excited, Mitchie bumped into a girl wearing designer labels top to toe. "Sorry, didn't see you," she said.

"Obviously," the girl said icily, turning away.

"That's Tess Tyler," said another camper. "Diva of Camp Rock. Her mother's TJ Tyler, rock goddess. I'm Caitlyn Gellar."

"Mitchie Torres," said Mitchie.

"I'm Caitlyn."

"Mitchie."

The big news going around camp was that the special guest instructor this year was **Connect 3's Shane Gray!**

The campers didn't know it, but Camp Rock was **NOT** the place Shane wanted to be. When he arrived, he ignored his uncle, Camp Director Brown Cessario, and headed straight for his room.

"What's the haps, Shane?"

After Mitchie had helped her mom by laying tables in the Mess Hall, she went up on stage. Thinking she was alone, she started to play the piano and sing a song called **This is Me**.

Shane was outside, hiding from his fans. Mitchie's lyrics really got to him, but by the time he got inside to find the singer, she was gone ...

★ **"Hello? Who's in here?"**

"I was in three music videos."

That night, Mitchie met Tess again, with her friends, Peggy and Ella, and cool reggaeton partners Barron and Sander.

"Hi, I'm Mitchie Torres," said Mitchie.

"Is your dad Nicky Torres, the composer?" asked Peggy.

"Er, no, he owns a hardware store," said Mitchie.

When she saw Tess roll her eyes, Mitchie made a split-second decision. I'm at Camp Rock, she told herself. Nobody knows me. I can be whoever I want to be! "Uh, my mom is, uh, president of **Hot Tunes**, China," she said. "I met all the stars there. Was in three music videos, too."

Tess smiled, impressed by Mitchie's lie. "Yeah?" she said. "There's an extra bed in our cabin. It's yours if you want it."

23

Mitchie moved into what Tess called the Vibe Cabin, and unpacked. The last thing she unpacked was the one thing she always had with her: her precious song book.

"Let's hear one," said Peggy.

Mitchie took a breath, then sang **This Is Me**.

"Totally good," said Peggy.

Tess nodded, and her lips turned up in a smile – but her eyes were icy cold. "Totally," she said.

"Totally good."

The next morning, Mitchie's alarm clock went off extra early, and she sneaked out to get to work in the kitchen while the others were still fast asleep.

No way were Tess and the others going to find out about her mom being the Camp Rock cook ...

Mitchie had made some great new friends — or had she?

Turn to **Chapter 3** on page 30 to find out!

Ready to Rock!

The Camp Rockers are ready to rock! These pictures look the same, but 10 things are different in picture 2. Can you spot them all?

Answers:

Camp Rockers!

Unscramble the names and write them on the lines, with each Camp Rocker's number.

1 RABRON **H**
Barron

2 LYCTIAN **C**
Caitlyn

3 LALE **G**
Ella

4 SOJAN **F**
Jason

5 IEMIHCT **B**
Mitchie

6 TENA
Nate

7 GYGPE **A**
Peggy

8 RENDAS **I**
Sander

9 NASHE **D**
Shane

10 SETS **E**
Tess

Answers: a-7 PEGGY, b-5 MITCHIE, c-2 CAITLYN, d-9 SHANE, e-10 TESS, f-4 JASON, g-3 ELLA, h-1 BARRON, i-8 SANDER, j-6 NATE.

Now find the names of the Camp Rockers in the word square.
They are spelled out from top to bottom, from left to right,
and from right to left. Draw a line through each name you find,
and tick ✔ the list.

E	T	A	N	O	P	B	S
S	E	C	X	L	P	A	M
H	S	A	N	D	E	R	I
A	S	I	V	W	G	R	T
N	K	T	A	O	G	O	C
E	L	L	A	M	Y	N	H
Z	Q	Y	B	Z	K	M	I
S	P	N	O	S	A	J	E

BARRON ✔
CAITLYN ✔
ELLA ✔
JASON ✔
MITCHIE ✔
NATE ✔
PEGGY ✔
SANDER ✔
SHANE ✔
TESS ✔

Answers:

E	T	A	N	O	P	B	S
S	E	C	X	L	P	A	M
H	S	A	N	D	E	R	I
A	S	I	V	W	G	R	T
N	K	T	A	O	G	O	C
E	L	L	A	M	Y	N	H
Z	Q	Y	B	Z	K	M	I
S	P	N	O	S	A	J	E

CHAPTER 3
Camp Rock Rocks

After breakfast, Brown Cessario arrived to teach the first music class. "Who's up to sing first?" he asked, pointing from one camper to the next. "Eenie, meenie, mynie ... you."

His finger pointed at Mitchie. "Me?" she said.

Brown nodded. "You."

"Me?"

"You."

"It's good."

Mitchie took a deep breath. "Who will I be, it's up to me," she sang, growing in confidence as her voice filled the room.

"Is that an original?" asked Brown.

"Yeah, it's my song," said Mitchie. "But it's not, it's just ..."

"No buts," said Brown. "It's good. Very good."

Tess stared hard at Mitchie. She did NOT look happy.

"You gotta sing with us at Final Jam, Mitchie," said Tess after class. **"Want in?"**

Mitchie had planned to sing solo rather than back-up, but now she made her second split-second decision.

"Yeah," she said. "I'm in."

"To win, we need Shane on side," said Tess. "Come on, let's sign up for all his classes!"

"I couldn't go near my breakfast."

Later, Mitchie was alone in the kitchen when Shane Gray walked in. She couldn't let him see her working there, so she put on a big chef's hat, and dusted her face with flour.

"You work here?" asked Shane.

"Yes," said Mitchie, hoping that he wouldn't recognise her as a camper.

He didn't. "I'm Shane," he said. "But I'm sure even the kitchen help knows that."

"Of course," said Mitchie. "Nice to meet you."

"Actually, it's not so nice," said Shane arrogantly. "My manager sent over my list of allergies, but since I couldn't go near my breakfast, I assume you kitchen people didn't get it."

Mitchie could not believe what she was hearing.

"You're kind of being a jerk," she said. "There's a way to talk to a person, **and that's not it**."

Shane was taken aback. "Um, well," he said, "I'll have my manager send it over again."

Then he was gone ...

Later, Brown caught up with Shane and asked him to explain why he had not turned up to teach his class.

"Look, I didn't sign up for this camp," said Shane angrily. "Get my agent on the phone."

Brown saw that Shane was troubled, and wanted to help. But Shane made it clear that he didn't want his uncle's help.

"What happened to you, man?" said Brown. "That guy on TV, that's not who you are. What happened to the kid who loved music? Stop acting like it's all about you."

"In my world, it **is** about me," said Shane coldly.

Brown sighed. "In **my** world, you are an instructor here," he said. "Hip hop dance class at two. **Be there.**"

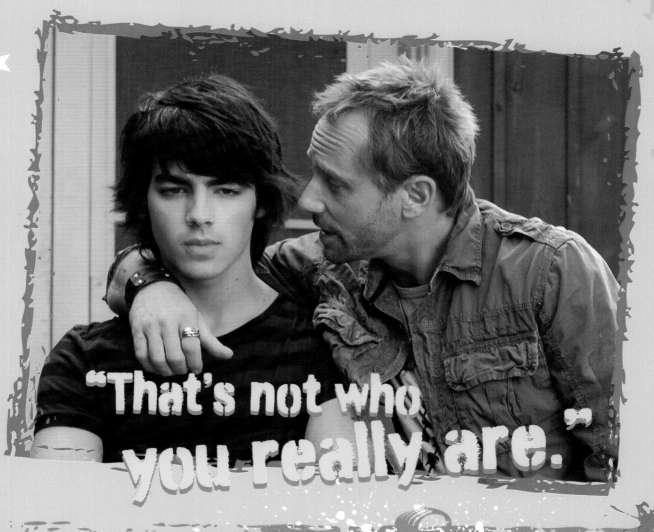

"That's not who you really are."

Later, in class, Shane played **Start the Party**. "Follow my moves," he said, then paused. **"If you can ..."**

"Five, six, seven, eight!"

That night, at the Campfire Jam showcase, Shane watched as the It Girls, Mitchie, Ella and Peggy, sang back-up for Tess on **I'm Too Cool.**

After the performance, Shane turned to go, but paused when he overheard two guys dissing Connect 3 as pop star garbage.

"They've totally lost it," said one, and his friend nodded ...

Would Shane change his arrogant ways?

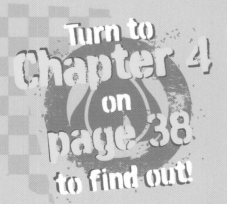

Turn to **Chapter 4** on page 38 to find out!

"**Shane Gray is so played ...**"

CONNECT 3s

Connect 3's Shane, Jason and Nate need to reconnect with their equipment. Can you untangle the cables for them?

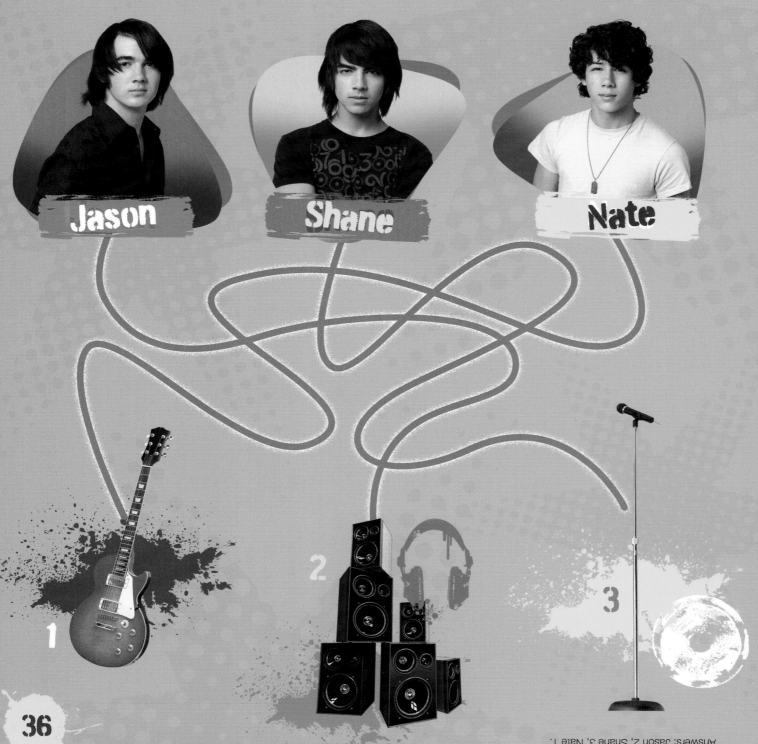

Jason

Shane

Nate

1

2

3

Answers: Jason 2, Shane 3, Nate 1.

Draw lines to connect 3 identical pictures of Connect 3's Shane, Jason and Nate.

Answers: Shanes 3, 8 and 10 are identical; Jasons 1, 6 and 12 are identical and Nates 2, 7 and 9 are identical.

CHAPTER 4
Second Chances

The next day, Mitchie walked down to the lake, and stopped to listen when she heard Shane playing guitar and singing outside Brown's cabin. "That was kinda different," she said. "I liked it."

"If you like stupid pop star stuff," said Shane.

"I thought you loved your sound," said Mitchie. "You created it here. You're like a **Camp Rock legend.**"

"Some legend," said Shane. "I just play the music the label thinks will sell. That's it."

"Some legend."

Mitchie smiled. "You don't think that song would sell?" she said as she turned to walk away. "I know one girl who would definitely buy it."

Later, Shane asked Mitchie to listen to a song he had written, **You're the Voice I Hear Inside My Head.** "I heard this girl singing and it reminded me of the music I like, so ..."

"It's really good," said Mitchie. "And I don't lie."

Shane smiled, and looked hard at Mitchie. "You seem different," he said. "Good different."

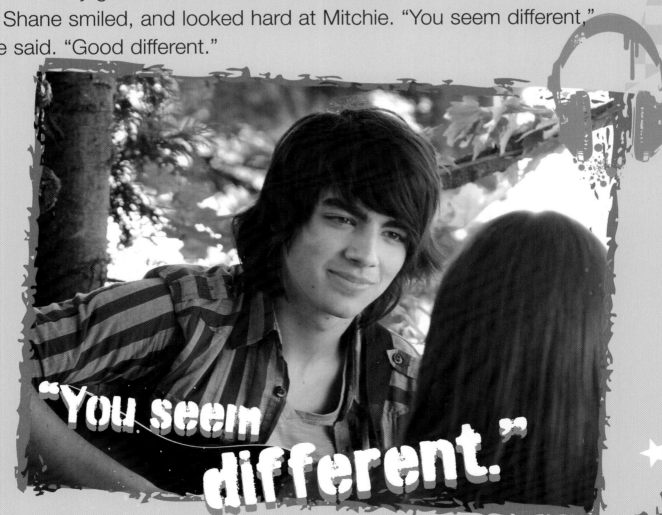

"You seem different."

That night, Caitlyn started a food fight with Tess, and Brown put her on kitchen duty as a punishment.

When Mitchie came out of the kitchen storeroom and saw Caitlyn chatting to her mom, she panicked, and hid her face behind a giant bag of crisps. But in her hurry to escape, she stumbled, and crashed to the floor ...

"Whoa!"

CRRUNCHH!

"Caitlyn, meet my daughter, Mitchie," said Mitchie's mom as she went out of the door.

"Mitchie? You're the cook's daughter?" said Caitlyn. "How long did you think you could keep up that lie about your mom being a big shot? Why did you say that?"

Mitchie paused, then shrugged. "I just wanted to fit in," she said angrily. "OK?"

"So? Go tell everybody!"

41

That night, when Caitlyn played at the Pyjama Jam showcase, Shane and the other campers watched and listened intently.

Tess didn't like that one little bit, so she put on a performance of her own. "Help!" she cried, pointing. "Help! Snake!"

When all eyes turned to Tess, Caitlyn stopped mid-song, her audience lost – and the 'snake' was nowhere to be seen.

Later, when Caitlyn spoke to her about what she'd done, Tess made **W E M L** hand signs: **What Ever Major Loser.**

Mitchie looked at Caitlyn. She was hurt, and it showed.

"**W E M L** is **SO** last year, Tess," said Mitchie, and Tess stalked off, leaving Mitchie and Caitlyn to share a look and a smile that said they were best friends again.

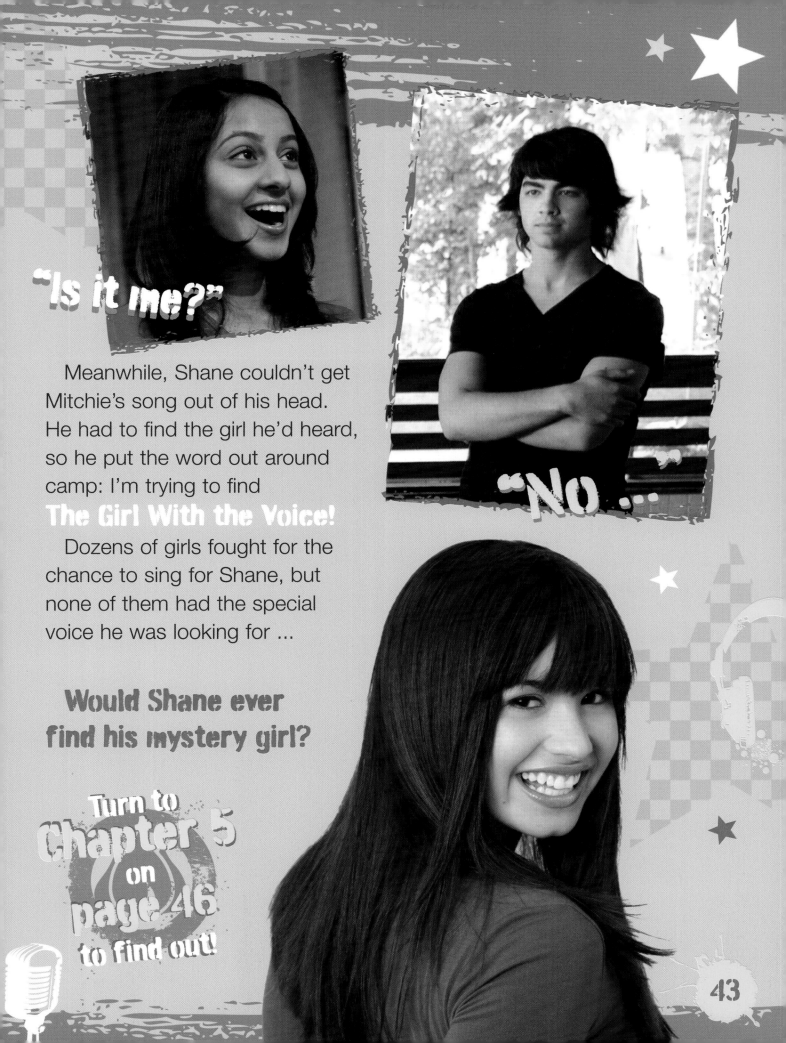

"Is it me?"

Meanwhile, Shane couldn't get Mitchie's song out of his head. He had to find the girl he'd heard, so he put the word out around camp: I'm trying to find **The Girl With the Voice!**

Dozens of girls fought for the chance to sing for Shane, but none of them had the special voice he was looking for ...

Would Shane ever find his mystery girl?

"No ...

Turn to **Chapter 5** on **page 46** to find out!

43

Favourite Things

It's all about you! Write a list of all your faves!

dream job

band

male singer

female singer

song

music style

album

Camp Rocker

clothes

pet

animal

meal

song

drink

film

hobby

magazine

colour

sport

film star

place

musical instrument

TV show

teacher

snack

name

friend

word

CHAPTER 5
The Girl with the Voice

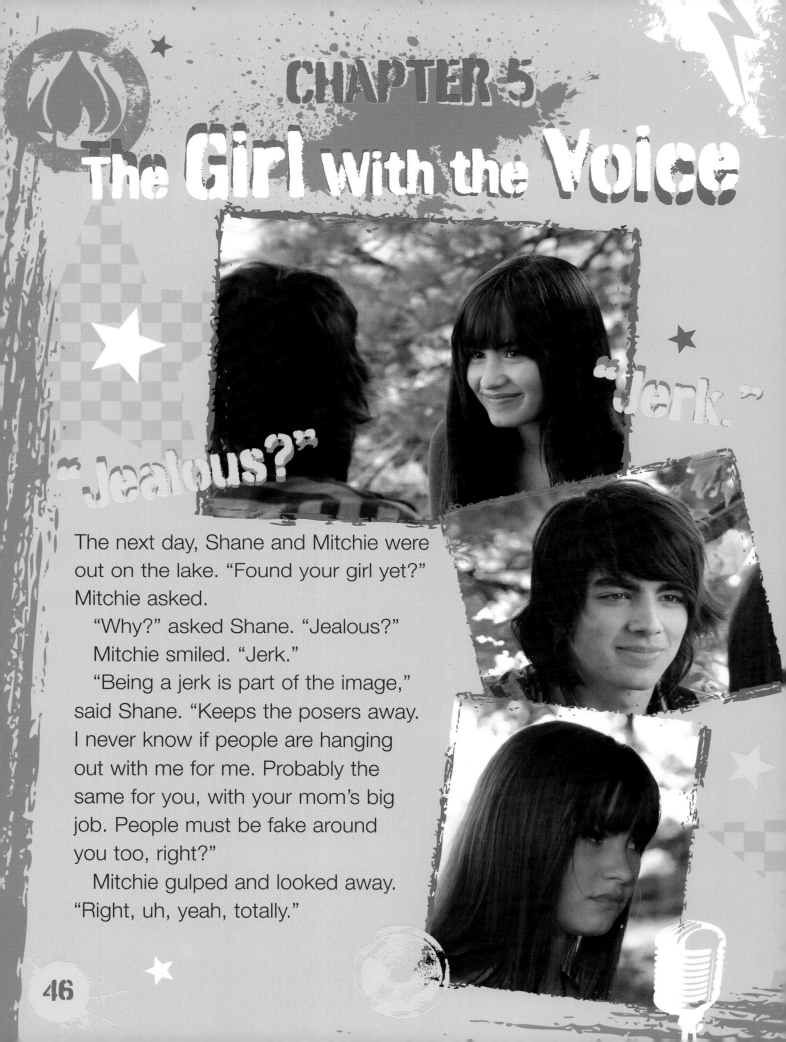

"Jealous?"

"Jerk."

The next day, Shane and Mitchie were out on the lake. "Found your girl yet?" Mitchie asked.

"Why?" asked Shane. "Jealous?"

Mitchie smiled. "Jerk."

"Being a jerk is part of the image," said Shane. "Keeps the posers away. I never know if people are hanging out with me for me. Probably the same for you, with your mom's big job. People must be fake around you too, right?"

Mitchie gulped and looked away. "Right, uh, yeah, totally."

Later, Tess saw Mitchie and Caitlyn leaving the kitchen. "Bye, Mom," said Mitchie. "We did the dishes!"

Tess smiled. So, Mitchie's mom was the camp cook, not a big shot in the music business? And Mitchie was the kitchen help? This was just too good to be true.

So that's who Mitchie is ...

Later, Nate and Jason arrived at camp for Beach Jam and **Connect 3** played Shane's new song, *Play My Music.* It was very different from their usual stuff but the campers went wild for it.

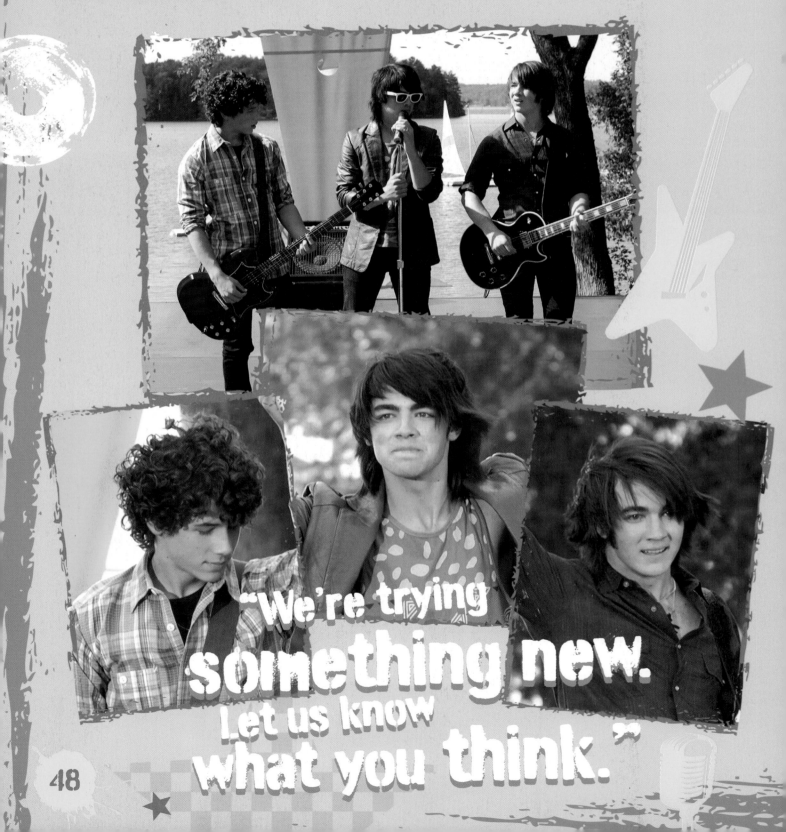

"We're trying **something new.** Let us know **what you think.**"

After the performance, Tess stopped Mitchie in the crowd. "Hey, tell us about your mom again," she said. "Just how important is she?"

Mitchie hesitated. "She ... uh ... well, she's not president of **Hot Tunes.** She's ... uh ... the cook here at Camp Rock."

"You lied to us?" said Tess.

The other campers overheard, and their faces said it all: **how could she do that?**

"You lied, Mitchie," said Shane angrily as he turned to walk away. "You're like all the others. You wanted to be friends with Shane Gray, not me."

"You were lying?"

The next day, Tess overheard Shane talking to Brown about the song he'd heard **The Girl With the Voice** singing. "This is real, this is me," he said. "I just can't get those lyrics out of my head."

Tess' eyes opened wide. She'd heard those words before! She went to the Vibe Cabin, and took out Mitchie's Songs from its hiding place. Yes, she was right. Mitchie was **The Girl With the Voice!** But no one was going to know that. No one ...

Mitchie ...

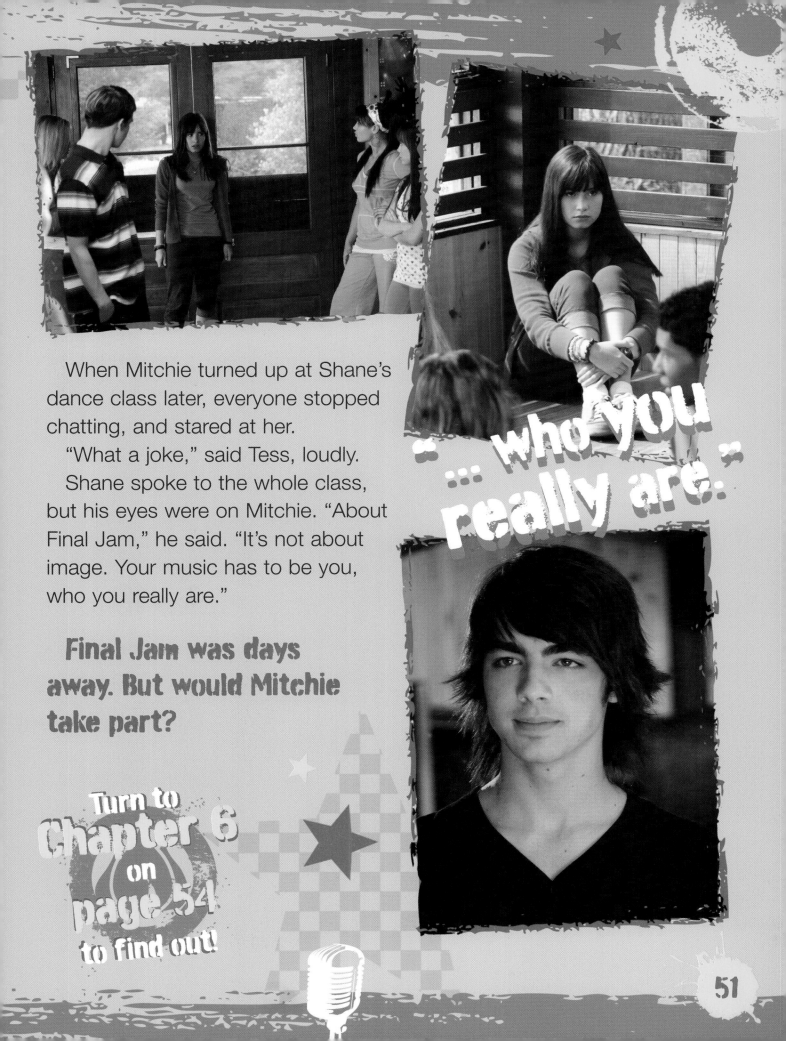

When Mitchie turned up at Shane's dance class later, everyone stopped chatting, and stared at her.

"What a joke," said Tess, loudly.

Shane spoke to the whole class, but his eyes were on Mitchie. "About Final Jam," he said. "It's not about image. Your music has to be you, who you really are."

Final Jam was days away. But would Mitchie take part?

Turn to Chapter 6 on page 54 to find out!

"... who you really are."

Rock On!

The one thing all the Camp Rockers want to take home with them – apart from a recording contract! – is a souvenir T-shirt. It's the year's fashion must-have!

Rate these T-shirt designs by giving each one a mark out of 10.

..7.../10

..9.../10

..9.../10

..10./10

..9.../10

Design and colour your own Camp Rock T-shirt.

Final Jam

In the days before Final Jam, eveyone practised like crazy.

Mitchie and Caitlyn were working in the kitchen when Brown arrived with Tess. "Tess says you two stole her charm bracelet," he said.

"**What?!**" said Mitchie. "No ..."

"She's lying," said Tess. "That's what she does."

"What?!"

"I know it was her."

But then Brown saw the bracelet poking out from under a cookbook. "Rules are rules," he said. "I gotta ban you until the end of Final Jam."

"But we didn't do anything," said Mitchie. "It's not ..."

"Sorry," said Brown. "You're both banned from camp activities until the end of Final Jam!"

"Rules are rules."

"We didn't do anything."

Before Final Jam began, Brown had news for the audience. "This year's winner gets the chance to record with Shane Gray," he announced to wild whoops and cheers.

"**Connect 3** will be the judges, so use your glo sticks to show them who you like!" added Music Director Dee LaDuke.

First on were Barron, Sander and the Hasta La Vista Crew, who brought the house down with their high-energy reggaeton moves and music.

"Who's stoked?"

"The Hasta La Vista Crew!"

Tess was next, but she was on her own, because Ella and Peggy had finally got tired of her diva ways and refused to sing back-up. She started well, but then she saw her mom take a phone call in the middle of her song. She stumbled so badly that the dancers had to help her off stage ...

Next up was Peggy, whose rocking, guitar-hero version of **Here I Am** brought the house down, and lit up the theatre with a sea of waving glo sticks.

When the applause finally faded, Brown leapt back on stage. "That's the end of Final Jam!" he yelled. **"THE END OF FINAL JAM!"**

As he spoke, Mitchie and Caitlyn walked on stage. They had understood Brown's message. Final Jam was over, and so was their ban!

Caitlyn played keyboards as Mitchie sang **This Is Me**. There was no costume. No image. No pose. This was the real Mitchie. Her words. Her music. Her feelings. Her voice. Herself.

Shane stared. **"That's The Girl With the Voice,"** he said, jumping up on stage.

"No more hiding who I want to be, this is me," Mitchie and Shane sang together. Their fingers touched, and they gazed deep into each other's eyes, and smiled ...

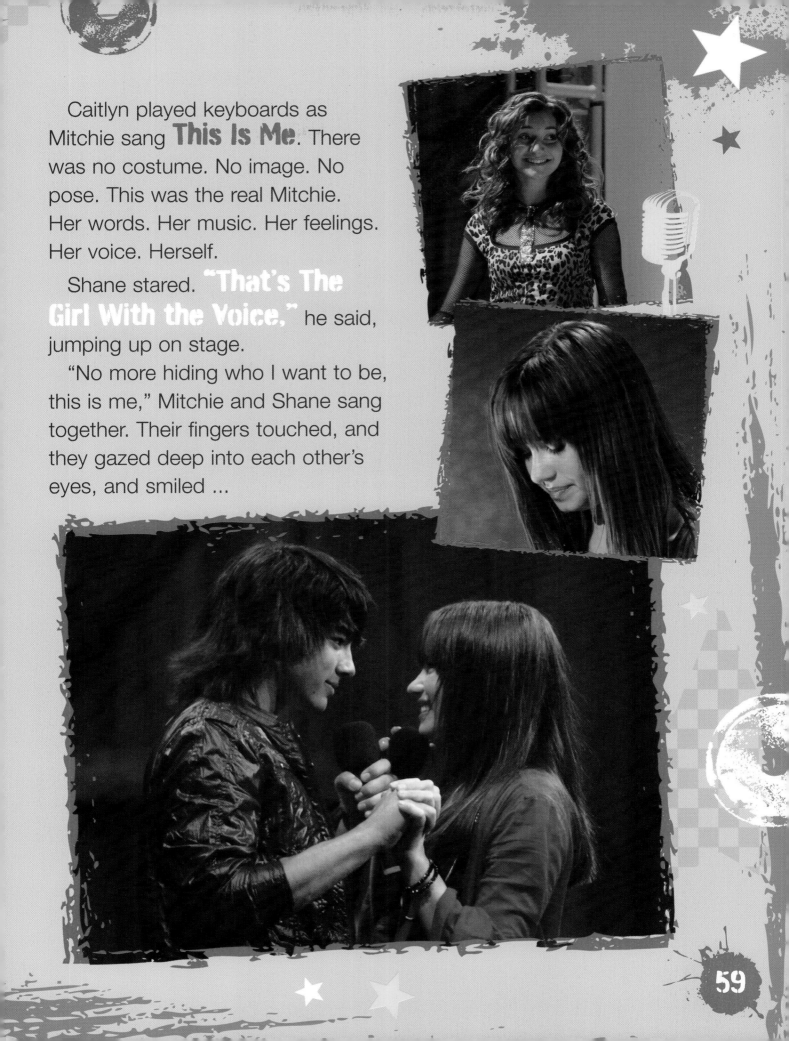

When Brown announced Peggy as the winner of Final Jam, the audience went wild, clapping and cheering.

While Shane posed for photos with Peggy, Mitchie and Caitlyn watched from the wings, where Tess found them.

She had lost her icy stare and her usual arrogance. "You two were great," she said, sincerely. "Look, I ... uh ... told Brown you didn't take my bracelet. See you next summer, maybe?"

Minutes later, Shane caught up with Mitchie backstage. "I guess my search is over," he said.

"Depends who you're looking for," said Mitchie. **"I'm Mitchie."**

"I'm Shane," he said.

"Hi."

"Hi."

Brown had one more announcement. "OK, Camp Rockers," he said. "It's finale time – **the jam session!"**

That was the cue for Shane, Mitchie and all the other performers to take to the stage one last time for more moves, more music – and one last song.

Loud. Raucous.

Rocking.

Real.

63

Get Creative!

Use a mix of letters, words, pictures, patterns and colours to design rockin' CD covers for Mitchie and Shane.

Camp Rock Questions

How big a Camp Rock fan are you? Answer these questions, then check your rating!

1 What is Mitchie's surname?

- [ ] **a** Torrent
- [✓] **b** Torres
- [ ] **c** Thomson

1 POINT

2 What did Tess accuse Mitchie and Caitlyn of stealing?

1 POINT

...... her charm bracelet ....

3 Blue Cessario is the Director of Camp Rock.

[ ] True or [✓] false?

1 POINT

4 What did Tess call her backing singers?

- [ ] **a** the It Band
- [✓] **b** the It Girls
- [ ] **c** the It-ettes

1 POINT

5 Who's missing from the **Connect 3** line-up?   **1 POINT**

Shane, Jason and ....Nate....

6 Who won Final Jam?   **1 POINT**

............Peggy............

7 What was the name of Barron and Sander's act?

✓ **a** Hasta La Vista Crew

☐ **b** reggaeton

☐ **c** Connect 3   **1 POINT**

8 When he was hiding from fans outside the Mess Hall, what song did Shane hear Mitchie singing?   **1 POINT**

....This is me....

Check your answers and your Camp Rock fan rating:

0-3 so-what fan   **6-7 semi fan**

4-5 so-so fan   **8 super fan**

Answers: 1. b, Torres; 2. her charm bracelet; 3. false, his name is Brown Cessario; 4. b, the It Girls; 5. Shane, Jason and Nate; 6. Peggy; 7. a, Hasta La Vista Crew; 8. This is Me.

A Message For You

Use this code to complete the message.

A	B	C	D	E	F	G	H	I
★	◯	🎧	⚪	🎤	+	🔺	◇	☆

J	K	L	M	N	O	P	Q	R
◯	🔊	🔺	◉	□	⚡	×	△	✈

S	T	U	V	W	X	Y	Z
⬜	🏃	🛡	★	◉	✈	⚡	⚡

Mitchie and Shane hope you enjoyed

<u>c a m p</u>

 as much as they did!

<u>R o c k</u>

Remember, always  your

<u>F o l l o w</u>

 and be

<u>D r e a m s</u>   <u>T r u e</u>

to

<u>y o u r s e l f</u> !

Answer: Mitchie and Shane hope you enjoyed CAMP ROCK as much as they did!
Remember, always FOLLOW your DREAMS and be TRUE to YOURSELF!

ADVERTISEMENT